first 100 words

sticker book

Add a star sticker when you have completed each page.

priddy books

Me

My body

head

shoulders

arms

hands

legs

feet

How many toes do you have?

eyes

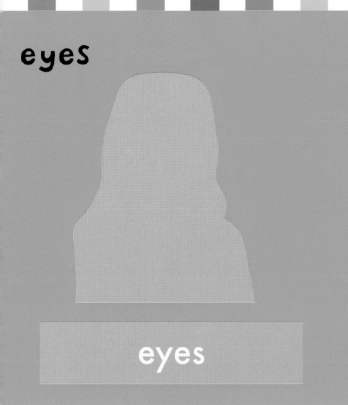

eyes

nose

nose

ears

ears

mouth

mouth

what color are your eyes?

3

table

table

chair

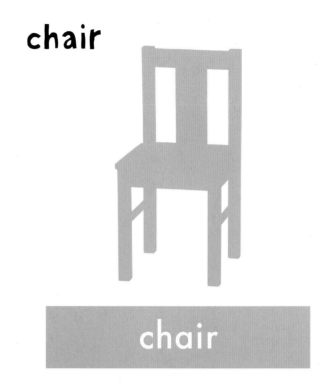

chair

cup

cup

bowl

bowl

What color is the chair?

spoon

spoon

sofa

sofa

picture

picture

clock

clock

What can you see in the picture?

ToyS

ball

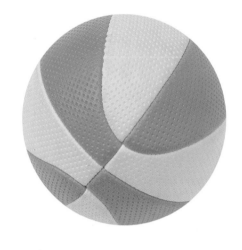

ball

car

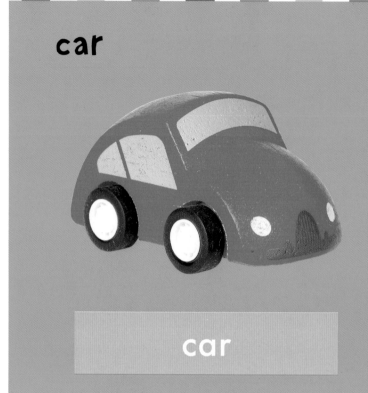

car

doll

doll

puzzle

puzzle

what noise does a car make?

blocks

blocks

teddy bear

teddy bear

pencils

pencils

airplane

airplane

How many pencils can you count?

apple

apple

cheese

cheese

tomato

tomato

juice

juice

Which one is a drink?

banana

banana

strawberry

strawberry

bread

bread

carrot

carrot

what color is the carrot?

Food and drink

jelly

jelly

butter

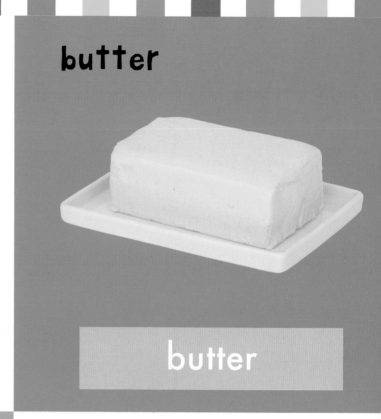

butter

pasta

pasta

orange

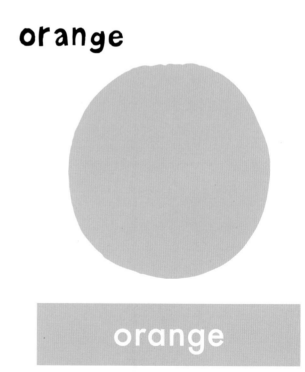

orange

which food is a fruit?

milk

milk

rice

rice

grapes

grapes

cookie

cookie

What shape is the cookie?

Clothes

socks

socks

T-shirt

T-shirt

pants

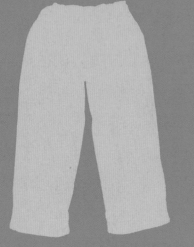

pants

sneakers

sneakers

What color are the sneakers?

hat

hat

dress

dress

coat

coat

shoes

shoes

What is spotted?

bathtub

bathtub

soap

soap

faucets

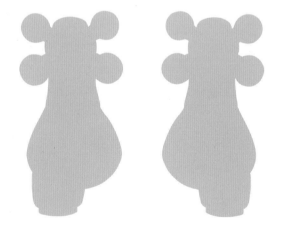

faucets

boat

boat

Which object is purple?

brush

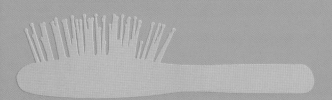

brush

rubber duck

rubber duck

towel

towel

toothbrush

toothbrush

Bedtime

slippers

slippers

bed

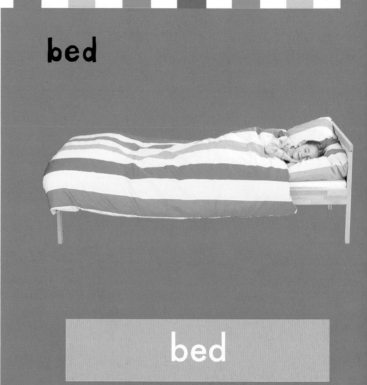

bed

pajamas

pajamas

blanket

blanket

where do you sleep?

teddy bear

teddy bear

lamp

lamp

book

book

pillow

pillow

what color is the lamp?

Colors

blue

green

blue	green

purple

orange

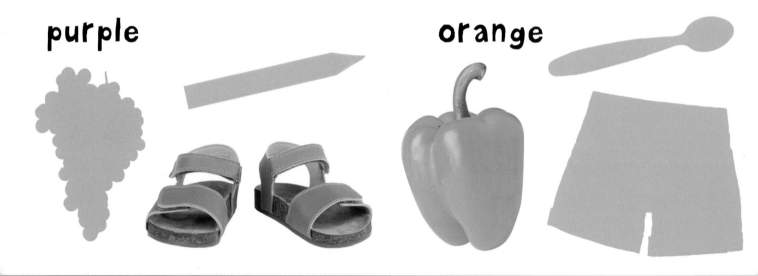

purple	orange

18

which shoes are blue?

pink

brown

pink

brown

red

yellow

red

yellow

which fruit is yellow?

Pets

fish

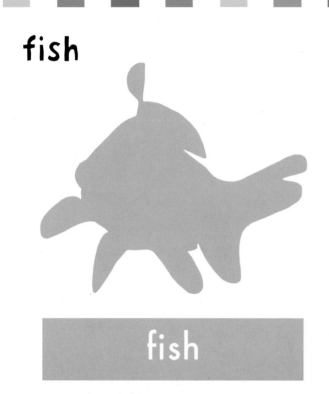

fish

dog

dog

kitten

kitten

rabbit

rabbit

What noise does a dog make?

parakeet

parakeet

puppy

puppy

guinea pig

guinea pig

cat

cat

Which pet can fly?

Outside

sky

sky

grass

grass

door

door

window

window

What color is the grass?

leaf

leaf

flower

flower

tree

tree

house

house

HOW many windows does the house have?

Farm animals

goose

goose

pig

pig

sheep

sheep

duck

duck

What color is the pig?

horse

horse

goat

goat

cow

cow

chicken

chicken

what noise does a cow make?

Farm babies

chick

chick

piglet

piglet

kid

kid

duckling

duckling

whose mom is a goat?

gosling

gosling

lamb

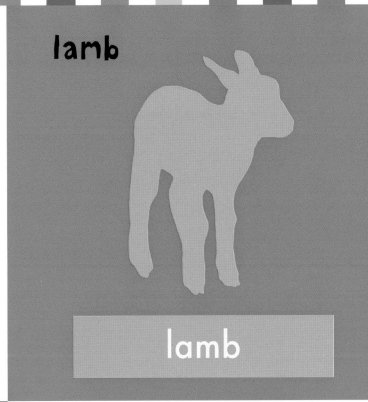

lamb

calf

calf

foal

foal

Which baby animal has a wooly coat?

Wild animals

tiger

tiger

elephant

elephant

snake

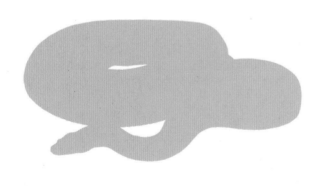

snake

bear

bear

Which animals have stripes?

hippo

hippo

lion

lion

chimpanzee

chimpanzee

zebra

zebra

What noise does a lion make?

Wild animals

butterfly

butterfly

camel

camel

sea lion

sea lion

fish

fish

30

Which animal has two humps?

squirrel

squirrel

giraffe

giraffe

lizard

lizard

penguin

penguin

which animal has a long neck?

Things that go

train

train

bus

bus

truck

truck

motorcycle

motorcycle

What noise does a train make?

car

car

boat

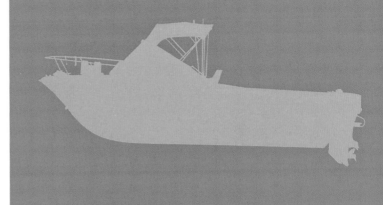

boat

tractor

tractor

bicycle

bicycle

who drives a tractor?

helicopter

helicopter

police car

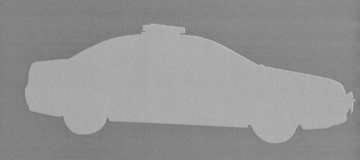

police car

digger

digger

race car

race car

What noise does a police car make?

airplane

airplane

ambulance

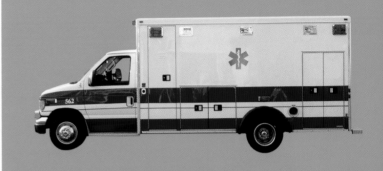

ambulance

scooter

scooter

fire truck

fire truck

who drives a fire truck?

Actions

laugh

laugh

talk

talk

drink

drink

eat
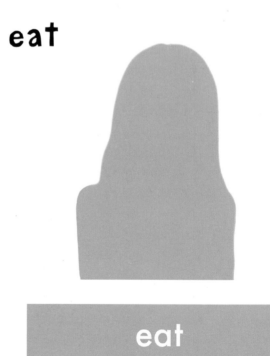

eat

Which child is eating a cookie?

sleep

sleep

walk

walk

jump

jump

play

play

Which child is in bed?

My house

window

car

door

tree

Find the word stickers, then complete the house picture.

ball

dog

flower

sky

In the park

grass

cloud

flower

boy

Find the word stickers, then complete the park picture.

girl

sun

bird

butterfly

In the city

bus

truck

man

woman

Find the word stickers, then complete the city picture.

car

scooter

house

bicycle

At the zoo

lion

tiger

camel

chimpanzee

Find the word stickers, then complete the zoo picture.

penguin

zebra

bear

elephant

On the farm

cow

duck

goat

pond

Find the word stickers, then complete the farm picture.

chicken

barn

sheep

horse

Shapes

rectangle

rectangle

circle

circle

triangle

triangle

square

square

What shape is a ball?

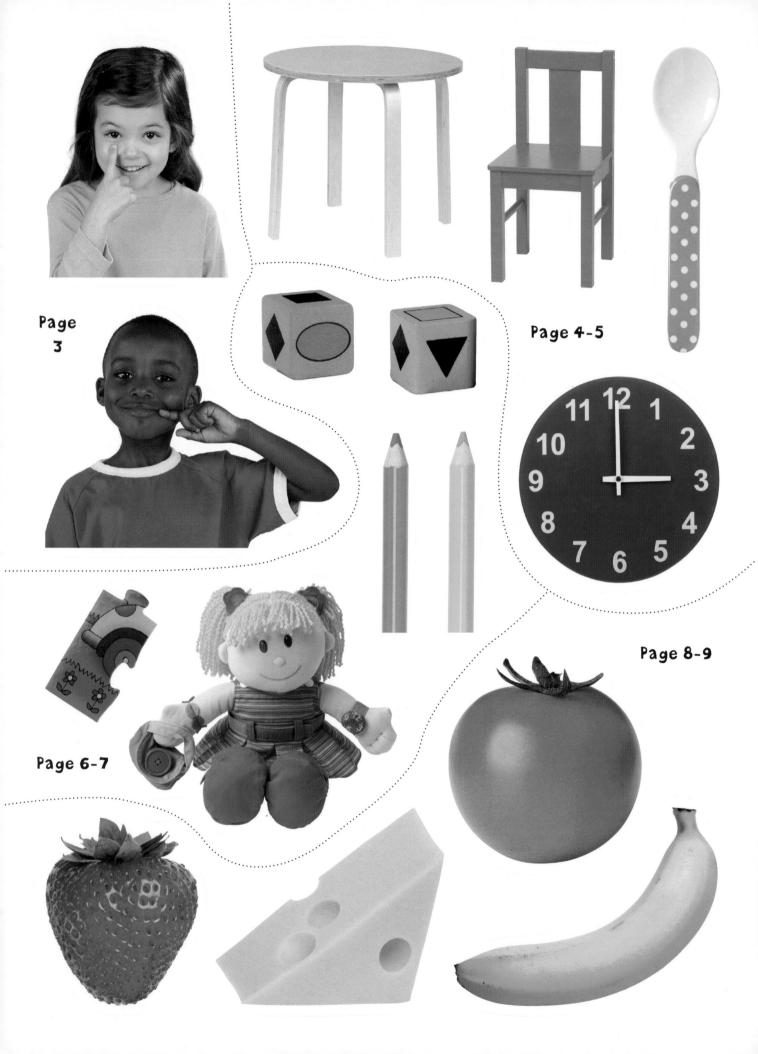

Me
Page 2-3

eyes

nose

mouth

shoulders

arms

hands

ears

legs

Inside
Page 4-5

spoon

chair

picture

bowl

sofa

table

cup

clock

Toys
Page 6-7

pencils

doll

car

puzzle

blocks

teddy bear

airplane

ball

Food and drink
Page 8-9

apple

bread

carrot

cheese

tomato

juice

banana

strawberry

Food and drink
Page 10-11

cookie

rice

grapes

jelly

butter

pasta

orange

milk

Page
10-11

Page
12-13

Page
14-15

Page
17

Page
16-17

Page 18-19

Clothes

hat

shoes

coat

pants

dress

sneakers

T-shirt

socks

Bathtime

soap

toothbrush

rubber duck

brush

faucets

boat

bathtub

towel

Bedtime

teddy bear

pillow

bed

book

lamp

blanket

pajamas

slippers

Colors

yellow

blue

purple

red

green

orange

brown

pink

Pets

fish

rabbit

cat

dog

guinea pig

parakeet

kitten

puppy

Outside
Page 22-23

door

flower

leaf

tree

house

grass

window

sky

Farm animals
Page 24-25

pig

goose

duck

sheep

goat

chicken

horse

cow

Farm babies
Page 26-27

gosling

duckling

kid

lamb

chick

calf

foal

piglet

Wild animals
Page 28-29

lion

zebra

bear

tiger

chimpanzee

hippo

elephant

snake

Wild animals
Page 30-31

giraffe

penguin

lizard

camel

fish

sea lion

squirrel

butterfly

Page
26-27

Page
28-29

Page 30-31

Page
36-37

Page
32-33

Page
34-35

My house
Page 38-39

ball

door

tree

flower

window

dog

car

sky

In the park
Page 40-41

flower

boy

girl

sun

cloud

butterfly

bird

grass

In the city
Page 42-43

bus

bicycle

woman

man

car

scooter

house

truck

At the zoo
Page 44-45

lion

chimpanzee

tiger

penguin

elephant

camel

bear

zebra